Andrew Adderup

Lincolniana, or the Humors of Uncle Abe

Second Joe Miller

Andrew Adderup

Lincolniana, or the Humors of Uncle Abe
Second Joe Miller

ISBN/EAN: 9783743420137

Manufactured in Europe, USA, Canada, Australia, Japa

Cover: Foto ©Andreas Hilbeck / pixelio.de

Manufactured and distributed by brebook publishing software
(www.brebook.com)

Andrew Adderup

Lincolniana, or the Humors of Uncle Abe

LINCOLNIANA;

OR THE

HUMORS

OF

UNCLE ABE.

Second Joe Miller.

That reminds me of a Little Story." — **PRES. LINCOLN**

By ANDREW ADDERUP, Springfield, ILL.

NEW YORK:

PUBLISHED BY J. F. FEEKS,

No. 26 ANN STREET.

PREFACE.

Is Joe Miller "complete?" I doubt it, maugre the pretenses of title-pages. An old joke is sometimes like a piece of painted glass in a kaleidoscope —every turn gives it a new aspect, and the new view is sometimes taken for the original phase. Perhaps this is true of some herein, although I am unconscious of that being so. If the accusation be made, try Uncle Abe first, for he is used to trials. As for me, I shall plead my privilege of telling you "the tale as it was told to me." But if these "little jokes" be not "sworn upon" for Miller, they shall stand for Uncle Abe—the writer hereof claiming only a godfathership. And others shall follow as fast as I glean them. To aid this purpose, let everybody who has a "good thing" send it to the publisher of this, and duly it will appear in the "complete" edition of Uncle Abe's jokes, always excepting the last, for the act of dying over will remind him of some little story with a *hic jacet* moral.

ANDREW ADDERUP.

Springfield, Ill., *April* 1, 1864.

LINCOLNIANA;

OR, THE

HUMORS OF UNCLE ABE.

An Involuntary Black Republican.

Sometime after Mr. Lincoln's well remembered passage of the rebel Rubicon at Baltimore, some radical Republicans, who thought they saw some signs of the President's backwardness in vindicating the Chicago platform, went in committee to the White House to beg him to carry out his principles—or rather to stretch them in Queen Dido's style.

"I don't know about it, gentlemen," replied Uncle Abe; "with a pretty strong opposition at home and a rebellion at the South. we'd best push republicanism rather slow. Fact is, I'm worse off than old blind Jack Loudermill was when he got married on a short courtship. Some one asked him a few days after, how he liked his new position. 'Dunno,' said he; 'I went it blind to start with, and ain't had a chance to feel my way to a conclusion yet.' So it is with me. Perhaps you can see further than I can to me the future is dark and lowering; and we have now got to feel every step of our way forward. Making Republicans used to be hard work, and I don't see as I could do much at it now, unless I proselyte by giving fat offices to weak-kneed opponents; but that," continued Uncle Abe, with a sly look toward several of his old Illinois friends, "would'nt be quite fair to those who believe that ' to the victors belong the spoils.' Your idea about pushing things reminds me of the first *black* Republican I ever made."

And the President threw his left leg over his right and subsided into that air of *abandon* which denotes his pregnancy of a good story.

"You see, gentlemen," he began, "in my boyhood days, I had a slim chance for schooling, and did'nt improve what I did have. Occasionally a Yankee would wander into Kentuck, and open a school in the log building that was a church and school house as well, and keep it till he got starved out or heard of a better location. One Fall a bald headed, sour-visaged old man came along and opened the school, and my people concluded I must go; as usual the big boys soon began to test the master, who, though he was a patient Jeffersonian Republican, seemed very tyrannical to us. My good nature singled me out soon, as the scapegoat of the school, and I got more than my share of the birch : at least, my back was as good as an almanac, for every day of the week was recorded there. But, though this record of past time was no pastime to me, I could stand it better than I could the taunts and jibes of the boys out of school.

" One morning when a half dozen of us were warming before the broad logwood fire, I noted a big fellow (who had got me flogged the day before) standing on the side opposite, his back to the blaze : both hands were partially open, one laid in the other ; some would lay it to the devil, but it was only the spirit of revenge which prompted me to pick up a live coal, covered with ashes, and drop it into his hands. For a moment he did'nt mind it, but it burned all the deeper ; when it did burn he jumped and bellowed like a stuck calf.

" ' Who made that noise ?' Demanded old Whitey, the master.

" ' I made it,' replied the big fellow, rubbing his hands.

" ' Why ?' more angrily demanded old Whitey.

" ' Some one put a coal of fire in my hand and burnt me,' sniffled the booby.

" The big fellow, however, didn't know who did it. Some of the boys, who had a lurking pity for me, said it snapt into his hand ; but the master " couldn't see it ;" and at last it leaked out that ' Abe Lincoln done it.'

" So you see, gentlemen," said Uncle Abe, moralizing, "I got the blame of a long score of supposititious shortcomings by one act of my own, pretty much as I had to bear the sins of my whole party in the late canvass, because of a few sins of my own."

" ' Abraham, come up here !' thundered the master, (By the way, gentlemen, my people always called me Abe—my wife still calls me plain Abe—but that old fellow called me *Abraham* so often and so severely that I early dropped all claim to a definite appella-

tive, and chose to be indefinitely 'A. Lincoln.')* But
to go on. I got a deserved threshing that time, and
a reputation withal for wickedness that saved all the
little rogues in school. At last, however, I determined
to be even with old Whitey, somehow.

"It wasn't long till I worked out an idea. Just
over the master's desk was a rude shelf, upon which
he kept some books and a big-bellied bottle of ink,
which some admirer of his Jeffersonian-Republican
principles had presented him. I had observed that in
stepping upon his desk platform, he never touched or
moved his chair, beyond leaning back in it, which he
always did, after taking his seat. So next day I
robbed our old long-tailed white horse of a few hairs'
and braided them in a three stranded cord. While the
master was gone out to his dinner, I put the thin
glass ink bottle upon the edge of the shelf propped
a-cant, and tied one end of the cord to the bottle, and
the other end to the back of his chair. The boys
sympathized with me, and were in an extacy of delight.
Anon the master came. Without looking to the right
or left, he marched sternly to the chair, and hence
saw not the repressed titter of expectation that was
ready to burst over the whole room. I stood just
outside of the door expecting the result; he sat down
and then leaned back. Down came the bottle, delu-
ging the bald head in a shower of Stygian blackness!

"Yes, gentlemen, I fancy that was the first *black*-
Republican ever made in Kentuck, but the conver-
sion was too sudden."

"How was that?" queried Cassius M. Clay.

"Why," replied Uncle Abe, "he afterwards married a widow and——twelve negroes."

*When Mr. Lincoln was nominated, very many papers ran up the name of Abram- Lincoln."

The Wrong Pig by the Ear.

I never knew a flash phrase worse used up than was one by Uncle Abe attending one of the neighboring Circuit Courts above Springfield. He was employed to aid a young County Attorney to prosecute some reputed hog thieves. The crime of hog stealing had become so common that the people were considerably excited and an example was determined on. The first person tried was acquitted on a pretty clear *alibi* or pretty hard swearing. As the fellow thus acquitted was lounging round the Court House, Uncle Abe was passing, and he hailed him.

"Well Mr. Lincoln, I reckon you got the wrong sow by the ear when you undertook to pen me up."

"So it seems," replied Uncle Abe, blandly, "but really you must excuse me, pigs are so very much alike! In fact, people up here don't all seem to know their own."

"Wilkie, where does Old Abe Lincoln Live."

In "Clay times," as the old farmers of Sangamon still recall the period of Henry Clay's powerful canvass for the Presidency, Uncle Abe had a wide circuit practice. In travelling to the various courts, he generally drove a horse and vehicle that some people will still remember. The horse had belonged to an undertaker, and the "funeral business," together with years, had made him a grave and staid animal. His *physique* presented those angularities that char-

acterized his master, but unlike his owner, he was
never known to perpetrate a joke or indulge in a
"horse laugh." The vehicle was neither buggy, nor
Jersey wagon, but had become, by virtue of alterations
and repairs, what Uncle Abe afterwards described
the Union under the plan of free and Slave States
"neither one thing or the other." There was in fact
an "eternal fitness" in horse and man that was not
exactly a "standing joke," but a peripatetic one.

I would give all my expectation of a brigadiership
for a portrait of Uncle Abe seated in this strange
"turnout," as he "might have been seen" wending
his meditative way across the prairies.

About this time Uncle Abe was nominated for
Congress in the Sangamon. Yet he did not forego
his business, but prosecuted his legal course, as well
as all evil-doers who chanced to fall into his hands.
He had just started on a circuit trip, to be gone a
month. Often, since Mr. Lincoln's nomination for
Congress, had Mrs. Lincoln begged him to add a
second story to their humble dwelling, but he
pleaded poverty. But a relation of Mrs. Lincoln's
having died in Kentucky leaving her a small
legacy, she determined her husband should have a
house worthy a candidate for Congress. Doubtless
she felt an inward satisfaction at the thought of fur-
nishing a good surprise for her husband on his return.
So she at once bought material, set mechanics at
work, and in three weeks metamorphosed the dwelling
into what political pilgrims to Springfield in 1860
will remember as a neat, two-story, clay-colored residence.

Uncle Abe arrived home just after dark, and drove

up to what he thought to be Eighth street, but not seeing his house, and thinking he had made a mistake, he drove round on to the next street. Recognizing the houses there; he again drove around to Eighth, and, passing his own house, recognized that occupied by W———n, a clever tailor, who was standing at his own gate.

"Why, is that you, Wilkie?" (said Uncle Abe patronizingly.) W———n, assured him of his own identity.

"Wilkie, where does Old Abe Lincoln live now."

"Well," said W———n, "The Loco's say he's so sure of his election that he's gone to Washington to select his seat; but Mrs. Lincoln lives now in that beautiful new two-story house you have just passed."

Uncle Abe indulged in a quaint laugh, and then turned his ancient horse around, alighted and asked if Mrs. Lincoln lived in the house before which he stood. Mrs. Lincoln received him as a fond woman should receive her lord, and the return was the cause of much pleasant badinage in social circles.

———

Too Literal Obedience.

Gen. McClellan was complaining to Uncle Abe of one of his division commanders, who had literally obeyed an order publicly given for the purpose of hood-winking the rebels through the aid of the numerous undetected spies known to lurk in the camp as well as the capital.

"That reminds me of a little story—a little thing

that happened to me when I was out in the Black
Hawk war," said Uncle Abe.

"You see, after we brought the Foxes to terms, they
were as sweet as wild honey. The women especially,
tried to make a good thing out of the defeat of their
braves, by selling us moccasins, deerskin breeches,
&c. One squaw in particular, made beautiful
breeches, and I concluded to have a pair made. How
she was to fit my spindles, puzzled me at first, as the
Indians are no tailors in any *measurable* degree. At
last I bethought me of an old pair which I had in my
saddle bag, and these I gave to her that she might
rip them open and use the parts for patterns. When
she brought the new ones home, I was not a little
angry to find that she had exactly imitated the old
patch on the nether parts of the new breeches."

Little Mac smiled in his peculiar grave way, and
remarked that when he gave an order for a similar
purpose, he would tell this story by way of a hint.

How Uncle Abe Felt.

Soon after Uncle Abe's defeat by Judge Douglas in
1848, (whereby Douglas unwittingly made a President) some one asked Uncle Abe how he felt over the
result.

"Well," said he, "I feel a good deal like a big boy I
knew in Kentuck. After he'd got a terrible pounding
by the school master, some one asked him how he
felt? 'Oh! said he, it hurt so awful bad I couldn't

laugh, and I was too big to cry over it.' That's just my case."

It is presumed the questioner got an idea how a defeated politician feels.

P. P. P.

Soon after the advent of Uncle Abe at the White House, the pressure of aspirants for official positions was perfectly crushing.

In fact, Uncle Abe sometimes got so flustered by their bedevilment, that he not only failed to recollect an illustrating anecdote, but soon lost his temper.

One of the Illinois applicants—a fellow named Jeff. D——r, was particularly a bore, seeming to think it part of the Chicago platform to give every village politician an office.

" Seems to me, Jeff," said Uncle Abe, " you got the Chicago platform reduced to enormous brevity—in fact, just three p's would seem to express your idea of it."

" How's that, Mr. Lincoln?" inquired Jeff.

" Why, it looks to me as if it was patriotism, place and plunder, and a mighty important plea is the last one, I reckon."

Jeff was silent for a while, but bored on until he "struck ile " in the shape of a clerkship.

Rattaned for a Rat Joke.

Just after the retreat of the rebels from Bull Run, when it leaked out that our troops had been held at bay by wooden or Quaker guns, a Pennsylvanian Congressman remarked to Uncle Abe—"Well, Mr. Lincoln, you see that Quaker principles even embodied in wood may be of some service in war."

"Yes, but as you see in that shape, they are only substituted principles; such things may do once, but found out, they will avail worse than nothing. Your remark, however, 'reminds me of a little story.'

"When I was a youngster of fifteen or so, I went to an 'Academy' for a few weeks, just to brush up my old-field school learning. Such schools are called Academies in the East, to distinguish their intermediate position between colleges and common schools; but in Kentuck and the West, generally the high sounding title merely meant that the 'principal' taught a few branches ahead of the old-field schools. Well, the rats were thick about the old building where we daily gathered to reap the fruit of knowledge; and as many of the boys brought their dinners and threw the fragments under their old-fashioned box desks, they soon grew as bold as they were thick. The teacher had a mortal antipathy to rats, and as I didn't 'take' to the teacher, I naturally encouraged the rats. Whenever one showed himself, he was sure to get a whack from the old teacher's rattan. Sometimes he missed his aim at the rats, but never at us boys, which was owing, perhaps, to the difference in the size of the game.

" An industrious rat had made a hole from beneath the floor up under my desk, and thence out through the end, and as I fed him well he was quite tame. Often during school hours he would come up and peer out into the aisles through his hole in the end of the desk, and whenever he was seen by the teacher, he was sure to see the rattan whirling in the air. An idea struck me one day. I got a dead rat—I did not like to kill my pet—and stuffing it, made quite a good-looking 'Quaker' rat. Then I fixed some springs so I could work my rat out and in at pleasure; so whenever the teacher was looking up, my rat was always out; but when the whack came down, he was in betimes. At last he seemed to think it wondrous tame, and the ill-suppressed titter of the school boys finally made him suspicious. The boys had been let into my secret, and relished it hugely, and I was too prone to give a few exhibitions. At last the teacher watched me sharper than he did the rat, and then caught me in the act. He got hold of the rat and beat me alternately with rat and switch, and you may well guess, I was well rattaned. If soldiers who use wooden guns ever get worse usage, I pity them."

The 300 Pounder Parrot since used by the Government, shows Uncle Abe's poor appreciation of Quaker guns and Quaker principles.

The State House Struck by Whiggery.

Soon after the State House at Springfield was

erected, in 1840, Mr. Lincoln stood on the east side of the Capitol Square one day, in conversation with a Democratic friend, who was loth to believe that the Whigs could carry the State for "Tip and Ty." "Nothing is more morally certain," said Uncle Abe. "All the signs of the times point to it, and—why even the State House is struck with Whiggery" he said, pointing up under the eves, where is yet seen a remarkable representation of a "coon" in the stone.

Graphic and True.

When Hon. Emerson Etheridge escaped from Tennessee during the summer of 1862, his opinions on Tennessee affairs were eagerly listened to in Washington. Among other questions, Uncle Abe asked :

"Do the Methodist clergy in your State take to secession ?"

"Take ? Why, sir, they take to it like a duck to water, or a sailor to a duff kid."

A Judge of the Post Office.

Judge David Davis of Bloomington, Illinois, who was recently appointed (by Uncle Abe) to a position on the bench of the Supreme Court of the United States, is known to many of his friends as one of the best hearted men in the world. His, is withal, full of the piety of good humor. I call it "piety," because I think a smiling face is a perpetual thanksgiving to God. His benevolence, however, edges down his wit, and gives it more the characteristic of humor, strictly speaking. This, while it may have helped that " belly with fat capon lined," has kept him at peace with himself and the world.

On one occasion, while Judge Davis was presiding at the Logan County Circuit Court, a case came up that involved a question of postal law. Uncle Abe was on the case, and politely loaned Judge D. a small manual of postal law, that he might see for himself what the letter of the law was. The Judge gave his understanding of the law, but had hardly finished when Mr. S———s, a burley farmer from Clear Creek, jumped up and sang out—

" I reckon that ain't so, Judge. I've been Post-Master more'n a dozen years, and I reckon I ought to know what's Post Office law."

Of course Judge Davis had every right to fine the man for contempt, but he had a different way of treating such cases. With a tone in which sarcasm only slightly blended, he said :

"Truly, I think you ought, Mr. S———s. It has never been my privilege to be a Post-Master, and I would like your opinion in this case. Please step this way."

The Judge moved over and made room on the bench, which Mr. S ———s occupied, and proceeded to give *his* opinion on the mooted question. The bar sat smiling in expectation.

" Keep your seat, Mr. S ———s, while I speak a word with my friend Parks."

Uncle Abe it was who had been interrupted, so he resumed

"May it please the Court, I had some doubt on this point myself, so I borrowed the usual manual of Postal Law, to be perfectly assured. I regret to contend that the clear letter of the law conflicts—sadly conflicts—with the view just taken by Judge S———s ; but "—

Here the bar indulged in a quiet " smile " without a stick in it, and it just popped into Mr. S———'s head, that he was out of place, and he skedaddled in haste.

" The largest *pussie* Judge that sat on our bench," remarked Will Wyatt. From that day to this, Mr. S———s, has never lost the title he so suddenly gained.

I 'm an Inderlid.

One day while Uncle Abe was attending to a case at Mount Pulaski, (the country seat of Logan County, Illinois,) he was beset by old B———s, a worthy farmer, but a notorious malaprop, for an opinion as to his amenability to the road tax. "You look here, Mr. Lincoln, these fellows here want to make me work on the road."

" Well!" said Uncle Abe.

" Well, I tells them that they can't do it, cause I'm an *inderlid*, you see."

(Of course Uncle Abe concurred in B———s opinion, and forgot to charge a fee.)

" On another occasion, he wanted John G. Gillette, the great cattle dealer, to *proximate* him because he'd got the best pair of cattle scales in Logan County."

How Uncle Abe got his Sobriquet.

Some one ventured to ask Uncle Abe, soon after his arrival at the White House, how he got the sobriquet of "Honest Abe."

"Oh," said he, "I suppose my case was pretty much like that of a country merchant I once read of. Some one called him a 'little rascal.' 'Thank you for the compliment,' said he. 'Why so?' asked the stigmatizer. 'Because that title distinguishes me from my fellow tradesmen, who are all *great* rascals.'"

"So honest lawyers were so scarce in Illinois that you were thus distinguished from them?" persisted the questioner.

"Well," quoth Uncle Abe, glancing slyly at Douglas, Sweet, and others from Illinois, "it's hard to say where the honest ones are."

"I'll take Number Eleven too."

Thirty-five or forty years ago, a trip from Sangamon or Macon County, to St. Louis, was an event to be talked of. It took as long to make it, and furnished food for as much rustic enquiry and comment, as does a voyage to Europe now. Uncle Abe had then given up rail-splitting, and was studying law. Having a little while before treated himself to a (then) rare thing, a suit of "store clothes;" and a neighbor being about to leave for St. Louis, he resolved to go along. As the teams toiled on at the rate of fifteen or twenty miles a day, they were gradually joined by others, till the train presented somewhat the sights now to be seen on our great overland routes to the Pacific.

On arrival at St. Louis, Abe determined to see high life, and accordingly made tracks for a letter A. No. 1, first class Hotel. The Old City Hotel was then the only house that could claim that distinction. There the merchants congregated, and there the Indian trader sought relaxation from frontier hardships, while the rough trapper was content with the humble fare of the "Hunter's Home."

I forget what association called out this reminiscence of that trip ; but there can be no harm in repeating the story. Such mishaps have befallen incipient greatness before.

At the dinner table, each waiter was provided with a wine card, and each guest had his wine charged to the number of his room, simply calling out, as for instance, Sherry No. 9, &c. A jolly Indian trader. sat just opposite Abe, who betimes called " Claret, No 11." Abe saw that most of the guests were similarly providing for themselves, and concluded not to appear penurious, so he said he'd take some wine too.

" What kind, sah ?" asked the waiter.

" Oh, I'll take the same,"—pointing to the bottle just called for by the Indian trader.

" What number, sah ?"

Abe was puzzled. He had not been used to wine or hotel life ; but it was only a moment before he broke the ice.

" Oh, I'll just take No. 11 too."

The trader looked up surprised, while several others near by, smiled a faint comprehension as to the state of affairs.

" Why, young man," said the trader, " that is my number, and mine is a single room."

" I beg pardon," stammered Abe, conscious that he had betrayed rusticity and ignorance ; but not knowing exactly how to extricate himself, the good-hearted trader came to his aid—

" Were you ever in the city before ?" asked he.

" Never before."

" Well, then, in memory of your advent, it shall be No. 11 too," and he quietly pushed the bottle across the table. So agreeable was he that Abe rallied, and the second bottle followed the fate of the first. On renewing the conversation after dinner, the trader was satisfied that Abe had 'lots' of 'horse sense,' but little of worldly experience, and he friendlily invited him to go out with him as a clerk; but, Abe declined. Had he gone—what? Perhaps he might have become a respectable Indian trader—perhaps he never had been elected President, and perhaps we would have had no rebellion.

A Severe Retort.

UNCLE ABE took a great liking to the late Col. Ellsworth, and afterwards did him the honor of making a Colonel of him. The rebel Jackson did the rest, but enough of that. Many of our readers will recall the slim, spruce figure of Col. Ellsworth as he paraded the

streets of Springfield, dressed in a unique Zouave
uniform, a mere boy in appearance. He was full of
animal spirits. He and Bob O'Lincoln were cutting
up didoes in the Law office of Lincoln and Hornden,
which greatly annoyed Uncle Abe, and he gently re-
proved them. Bob, a little nettled, replied by quoting
the common couplet :

> "A little nonsense now and then,
> Is relished by the wisest men."

"Yes," said Uncle Abe, looking severely at Bob,
"that's the difference between a wise man and a fool
who relishes it all the time."

Bob subsided, and Ellsworth betook himself anew
to Blackstone.

Had all the Time there Was.

When Uncle Abe used to attend the Courts in the
regions round about Sangamon, he generally made
easy stays, and was wont to look at the country and
talk to the people at his leisure. On one occasion he
was riding by the premises of old H———, who was
notorious for his unthriftiness, and who was in the
act of driving some stray hogs out of his corn-field.

"Good morning, Mr. H———," said Uncle Abe.

"Morning, Mr. Lincoln, morning."

"Why don't you mend that piece of fence thoroughly, Mr. H———, and keep the pigs out?" asked
Uncle Abe.

"Ha'n't got time," said H———.

"Why," said Uncle Abe, with   air of blended

reproof and humor, " you've got all the time there is Mr. H———."

Whether H——— mended his fence and his thriftless habits, this deponent knoweth not ; but has often thought how true was the remark, whether as a joke or an admonition. Every second, minute or hour is ours—ours to use or ours to squander. How wontonly wasteful would be the rich man who should stand upon a vessel's deck and cast his million golden coins into the sea ; yet day after day we stand upon the shores of eternity, and cast the golden moments into the unreturning past. All the knowledge and wealth of the world is but the result of improved time. So don't say you "havn't got time," for you've got all there is, as Uncle Abe says.

Could Stand it a Day or Two.

About the time this occurred, there stood on one side of Capitol Square, in Springfield, a Hotel, now doubtless out of memory of most of the occupants of the out-lots and additions which speculators have hitched to the original village. In its day it was a "first-class hotel," but it waned before the "American" and is now among the "things that were." There were some who doubted the clenliness of the *cuisine*, and "thereby hangs a tale."

Judge Brown arrived in town and put up at the aforesaid hotel, whereat, Uncle Abe, on meeting him, expressed his regret, begging him to become *his* guest. The Judge would fain not trouble his friend.

" But you know the reputation of the place—the kitchen?" said Uncle Abe.

" I've heard of it," said the Judge ; " but as I want to keep my appetite, I always shun the kitchen, if not the cooks."

"But surely, can't you see by the table alone, Judge?"

" I know, Mr. Lincoln, but I'm going to stop only a day or two, and I guess I can stand for that time what the landlord's family stand all their lives."

Speaking of Hotels, reminds me of a little episode of one of Uncle Abe's professional visits to Cairo, in Egypt, a town fenced in with mud-banks and celebrated for its mud-holes and mean whisky. Thereabouts is a Hotel, and thereat Uncle Abe stopped ; because the water forbade further traveling. When his bill was presented to him next morning, he ventured to remark, " that his accommodation had not been of the most agreeable kind."

" We are very much crowded," apologetically replied the landlord.

"But I had hard work to get breakfast this morning."

" Yes," continued the apologist, " we are greatly in need of help."

" Well, well," said Uncle Abe, " you keep a first rate hotel in one respect."

" Ah!" said the landlord, brightening up, " in what respect is that?"

"Your bills," said Uncle Abe, vanishing towards the "Central" cars.

The Ky-ro-ite landlord perhaps thought he ought to be well compensated for keeping a hotel in such a place. A man of his sort used to "keep tavern" in Pasy County, Indiana, several years ago. A pedestrian stopped with him over night, for which the charge was $2.50.

"Why, landlord," said he, "this is an outrageous bill."

You mean it's a big 'un ?" said the insatiate Boniface.

"Yes, I do."

"Well, stranger, we keep tavern here."

"What has that to do with such a bill?"

"Look at that 'ere sign, stranger—cost ten dollars; your'n the fust trav'ler that's bin along for three weeks, and we can't afford to keep tavern for nothin'—*we* can't!"

Not the Worst of It.

Gov. Morgan, of New York, was urging the employment of General W——— in active service. Seward objected, that he was "too old" for the emergency of the times.

"Yes," said Uncle Abe, "we've got too many old officers in the army, and that is not the worst of it—*we've got two many old women* there!" This was when Uncle Abe's faith was strong in little Mac.

"Nobody Hurt."

"Some conclusions," said Uncle Abe on one occasion, "are nonsequential. To say that Rome was not built in a day, does not prove that it was built in a night."

Accoutred en Militaire.

In the outset of the famous Black-hawk war in Illinois, a "hoss company" was raised in the region where Uncle Abe was (then) a rising lawyer. I say rising, although he had then reached a height sufficient to help himself to most blessings—and he, the aforesaid U. A., was chosen Captain. Uncle Abe rode a "slapping stallion," who was either naturally restive, or appreciated his new honor too highly—at any rate, he corvetted and pirouetted like a very Bucephalus. At last he unhorsed his rider, who landed sprawling on the prairie in one of those green excrescences that abound where bovine herds range. As the discomfitted Uncle Abe rose, and surveyed his predicament, old Pierre Menard, who was a near spectator, remarked in his broken French :

"Vell, I nevair sees any man accoutred en militaire like zat before."

Most old suckers pronounce accoutred as the Yankees do the word cowcumber, and this rendered Menard's joke more unctious.

Perils of Illinois Lawyers.

Years ago, when the capital of Suckerdom was a

village of less " magnificence " than it now presents—
when Lincoln, Harden, Baker, McDougal, Douglas,
Shields and Ferguson were all village lawyers, and
scarcely known to fame—Judge Thomas Brown was
on the Supreme bench of the State.   He was to some
extent a " character ;" but not a very successful
lawyer.   He went to California, since when he has
been generally lost sight of; but his old friends may
be assured that if he is in the "land of the living,'·
Uncle Abe's tax collectors will find him.   But that's
neither here nor there.   His ideas of the perils of
practicing law in Illinois, in early times, is what is
now before the reader.

On one occasion, after he had changed his residence
to Peoria, having some business to transact in Springfield, he arrived in that place and put up at the old
American House, (now kept by Henry Ridgely, Esq.)
He chanced to mention the name of Peoria.   In-
stantly the attention of a countryman was fixed
upon him, who, at the first opportunity accosted
him—

" From Peoria, Squar ?"

" Yes."

" Much acquainted ?"

" Pretty well, Sir."

" Know a lawyer up there named **H——g R——s** ?"

" Yes sir."

" How's he getting along ?"

" Oh, first rate—devilish lucky man."

" He's getting hold of considerable land, hain't
he ?"

" Yes a deal—devilish lucky man.

" Yes—large—devilish lucky man."

"Look here, Squar," said the countryman, evidently puzzled at R——s being so devilish lucky, "What do you mean about his being so lucky?"

"Mean? why I call any man lucky that practices law twenty years in Illinois, and don't get into the penitentiary."

Couldn't Make a Presidential Chair.

"Mr. Lincoln," said an ardent sovereignty man just at the beginning of the last Presidential contest "Mr. Douglas is a cabinet maker."

"He *was* when I first knew him," said Uncle Abe, "but he gave up the business so long ago, that I don't think he can make a Presidential chair now."

Uncle Abe proved himself a prophet, although at a tremendous cost to the country.

"Couldn't see it in that Light."

A delegation of temperance men recently sought to influence Uncle Abe to take some stringent steps to suppress intemperance in our armies. Among other reasons urged, they said our armies were often beaten because of intemperance.

"Is that so?" said Uncle Abe. "I've heard on all sides that the rebels drink more than our boys do, and I can't see why our boys, who drink less, are more liable to get whipped."

"But you know the corrupting influence of the army in regard to drinking habits," pursued the Committee.

"I've heard that, too," said Uncle Abe, "but I think they will do pretty well *if I can keep them out of Washington !*"

The Committee didn't carry their measure, by a jug full.

Too Tough for the Rebels.

When the Illinois boys gathered at Springfield, under the call of the ten regiment bill, they were quartered on the fair grounds, just out of the city. All the stalls were filled with troops, before which were signs as "St. Nicholas," "Richmond House," etc., etc. Charley W——, on going through the fair grounds, looked into the "Richmond House," and said—

"Well, boys, how do you get along?"

"Oh, first rate," replied the Chicagoians, " we're all *stall fed.*"

"Bully for you," said Charley; "hope you'll be too tough for the rebels."

Little Mac Helped by an Illustration.

"I can't seem to reap any advantage from the rebel movements," said McClellan, in consultation with Uncle Abe.

"Oh, you just keep a watchful, careful eye on Lee, and perhaps you will yet see how to make use of them, as old Mother Grundy did of her crooked wood."

"Thereby hangs a tale," remarked little Mac, with one of his peculiar, quaint smiles.

"You're right, General. Your remark reminded me of a good old neighbor of my father's, in Kentucky, who died many years ago. She was sweet-tempered—few such in this world." Uncle Abe stopped as though a mental comparison had damaged some woman of his acquaintance. "Yes, her disposition was of that kind that extracts 'good from things evil.' And she was her husband's pride and boast. One day he was praising her to a neighbor."

"'Look here, old man Grundy,' said the neighbor, 'these women are just like cats—they are all right as long as you stroke the fur the right way, but reverse the movement, and you'll see the fire fly. Now, I'll tell you what, I bet a four-gallon keg of my four-year-old peach, that I can tell you how to make her as mad as a set-hen, if you dare to try.'"

"'Done,' cried old man Grundy."

"'Well, you just haul home all the crookedest sticks of wood you can find, and then see.'"

"Old man Grundy brought home a small load every day or two, and it was knotty and crooked as a pigstail; but not a word or look of complaint. For a week this continued, with the same result, when he asked the good wife how she liked the wood."

"'Oh, 'tis beautiful wood,' said she; 'it burns

"Piled High with difficulties."

finely, and then it fits *around my pots and kettles just as if 'twas made on purpose.'*

Lee did not fit into Mac's hand so well, yet the story was not without its use to him.

An Acre of Fight.

During the progress of the Senatorial campaign between Douglas and Lincoln, Uncle Abe came home to recreate a few days. Douglas, long used to the political arena, bore the fatigues of the canvass like a veteran. His custom was to bathe just after supper, getting some friend to rub him like a race horse, when he would sit down and enjoy his whisky and cigar. Lincoln, lank and abstemious, bore his yoke with evident weariness. But to the story.

Uncle Abe went up into the Governor's room in the State House, where he was soon joined by many of the leading Republicans of the town. Some one remarked on his look of weariness. "It is a mighty contest," remarked Uncle Jesse Du Bois.

"But Mr. Lincoln does not show his great appreciation of it upon the stand," remarked a Chicago correspondent, in allusion to Uncle Abe's good humored replies to Douglas.

"But still, when the day's gladiatorial combat is over, it seems to me, as the Kentucky fellow said, that I had been through 'an acre of fight.'"

"Give us that story, Abe," said Dr. Wallace, Uncle Abe's brother-in-law.

"Well, one of my earliest recollections of a Kentucky Court, was a trial about a fight. It took place in the Court House grounds, and the Judge, thinking it constructable as a contempt of Court, sent out the Sheriff, and had the parties quickly brought before him. Both had bruised noses and beavers, and showed the unmistakable evidence of having been in a scrimage. The witnesses were numerous, and the evidence was so conflicting, that the Judge declared he could legally reach no other conclusion than that there had *been no fight at all*. But the Sheriff ventured to suggest:

"Here's Jim Blowers—he had hold on one of them fellers, when I arrested them."

"Mr. Clerk," said the Judge, "you will at once swear Mr. Blowers."

"Now, Mr. Blowers," said the Clerk, "you will please tell the Court what you know about this affair."

"Well, ax on."

"Well, was there a fight between these parties?"

"Just a bit of scrimage."

"It was a real fight, was it?"

"Well, some people would call it that."

"How much of a fight was it?"

"Oh, considerable—they pulled and hauled about kinder like two cows when they lock horns."

"But, tell the Court more precisely?"

"Well, I should say it was a right smart fight."

"But *how* much of a fight?"

"Well, then, just about an acre, I reckon."

It is needless to say that the crowd enjoyed the joke hugely.

———

"It is easier to pay a small debt than a larger one."

Uncle Abe Believes in the Intelligence of Oysters.

In the year 1860 or thereabouts, when a great patent case was being tried in Chicago, and champagne and oysters were the favorite viands served nightly to Counsel and Jurors after the adjournment of Court, it happened that one Ed. D——n, a young patent lawyer from New York, was present on one of those occasions. Now, Ned is terribly afflicted with a determination of words to the mouth, and managed to monopolize the whole conversation. Ned had a speech to make upon everything, and kept buzzing around like a musquito, dipping his bill into everything animate or inanimate, no matter which. At last he began to officiate at serving out the oysters, and with ladle in hand, said in his usual stilted style, " I wonder whether this bivalve, this seemingly obtuse oyster, is endowed with any degree of intelligence." Uncle Abe looked at the puppy, who, by the way, had prevented him cracking a single one of his favorite jokes for the entire evening, and quaintly remarked, that " he was satisfied that an oyster knew when to shut up, and that was more than some New York lawyers knew." Ned has never propounded the query as to the intellect of oysters since.

An Egyptian Snake Story.

The last county made in Illinois—I don't mean by

the Legislature, but by Nature, and where dirt was so short that it lies under water part of the year—is called Alexander, and used to boast two rival towns, both thoroughly Egyptian in their nomenclative association—Cairo and Thebes. Twenty years ago Thebes was the "seat of justice;" but Cairo was then beginning to entertain magnificent expectations, and her citizens wanted to have the Court House removed to their town. The contest waxed warm. The Thebans contended that Cairo was only a "daub of mud on the tail of the State," while Thebes was destined to hold the same relation to Alexander, that its ancient namesake did to Egypt in the time of Menes. [See Herodotus.] But to settle the dispute, the Legislature must be appealed to, and that involved the choice of a man favorable to the change. This narrowed the fight right down to a hot county canvass between the Theban and Cairoine interests.

A Cairo man conceived a scheme that was ahead of anything yet achieved by Uncle Abe's brigadiers in the way of "strategy." He wrapped a boulder in a green hide, making a perfectly round mass, to which he attached a mule ; then night after night he drew the stone through sand and mud. By going on a straight line, the mule's tracks were concealed, and the track left, resembled that made by a huge serpent. These tracks were mainly in the south end of the county, and caused an excitement that almost absorbed the election interest. Soon it was reported that Mrs. so and so had seen a huge snake. The wonder grew apace. Anon it was currently reported that two men had seen the great serpent five miles above Cairo. The excitement increased. Several daring hunters followed the track, of which new ones were made every night; but the trail always led into water and was lost. Several persons missed hogs and calves, which were surmised to have gone into the capacious maw of the serpent. Finally word was given out that a great hunt was to come off in the lower part of the county, and the rendezvous was appointed. On the morning, hundreds were there from all parts of the county, and dividing into squads they started to scour the country about. At night they returned from their snakeless hunt, but so anxious were the people to get rid of his snakeship, that they furnished an abundance of edibles and whisky. All were in hilarious spirits, determined to renew the hunt on the following morning. By daylight the hunters were again on the tramp, and men from the lower part of the county happened to fall into the squad.

About 3 o'clock in the afternoon, a squad of The-bans hove in sight of a small village, *i. e.* one house, a blacksmith shop and a grocery, where, seeing a large crowd assembled, they hurried up in expectation of seeing the dead monster. *But the men were voting !*

"Thunder!" cried a Theban, "this is election day, and I'll bet my bottom dollar we 're sold!"

They started for the rendezvous and spread their suspicions; but so few reached their own precincts, that the Cairo man was elected.

Then the joke came out; but the Thebans couldn't see the "laughing place;" their rage and mortification was so intense.

Uncle Abe was a member of the Legislature, when an effort was made to change the county seat of Al-

'exander; and though he liked the joke hugely by
which the Thebans had been "diddled," he saw the
honesty of the thing and so voted against any change.

Why Uncle Abe Made a Brigadier.

When the rebellion had gone so far as to give the
most hopeful some clear idea of its extent and malig-
nancy, it chanced that J. A. Mc——d, a leading politician of Illinois, made a visit to Washington, and
imitated his friend Douglas so far as to call upon
Uncle Abe. The "shoot" that certain prominent
Democrats gave indication of taking, by talking of
reconstruction and a Northwestern Republic, gave the
new administration some concern. Uncle Abe was
very sociable with Logan, Mac, and a few of their
"ilk." So Uncle Abe not only extended to Mac the
hospitalities of the White House, but accompanied
him on a visit to the arsenal. While there, their attention was drawn to some muskets which the speculators had furnished to Cameron, and which were
thought (generally) very dangerous to those who used
them.

Mac caught up one, and sighted along the barrel.

"Do that again, Mac," said Uncle Abe.

Mac complied. Uncle Abe was evidently struck
with an idea, and Mac was anxious to know what it
was like.

"Why, Mac," said Uncle Abe, "I was thinking if
we could get all our soldiers to make up that kind of

GREAT SNAKE SCARE IN EGYPT.

"By going on a straight line, the Mule's tracks were concealed, and the track left resembled that made by a huge Serpent."

a face, that the rebels couldn't stand it a moment."

Mac didn't relish Uncle Abe's joke, as he was hopefully in pursuit of the third wife ; but he put the best face he could upon the matter, and remarked to Uncle Abe—

"Perhaps you'd better make me a Brigadier then!"

"And why not?" asked Uncle Abe.

Mac got his commission.

Uncle Abe Puzzled.

Uncle Abe was met one day near Springfield, by a conceited coxcomb, who had built him a house at some distance, and invited him to dinner. Uncle Abe did not much relish the Jackenape's acquaintance. In fact, as Justice Shallow has it, had " written him down an Ass." However, Abe enquired very minutely, where Snooks lived? "Thistle Grove," replied the verdant Snooks; "but there's no grove now, and not a single thistle!"

"Eh, what!" cries Uncle Abe, "not a single thistle! Then what on airth do you live on?"

Uncle Abe Divided on a Question.

In 1840 or '41, Uncle Abe was a member of the Illinois Legislature. The Capital had lately been removed from Vandalia to Springfield. The Legislature met in the Presbyterian church.

J have forgotten what measure was before the house; but it was one in which there were many members who did not wish to commit themselves. Uncle Abe was in this predicament. He sat near an open window, and when the clerk, calling the ayes and nays had got down to L's, Uncle Abe thrust his right leg out of the window, and was just drawing its long companion after it, when an anti-dodging member " seeing the game," shut the sash down and held Uncle Abe in a trap.

" Lincoln," called out the Clerk.

" Mr. Speaker," said Col. Thornton, " Mr. Lincoln is *divided* on this question, and I move you that the sergeant at arms be sent to bring in that part of him that is out of the window."

Uncle Abe was " *brought in* " amid a universal titter, to his evident mortification.

In 1840, the Union generally went for Harrison; but Illinois, particularly, was democratic. When the Legislature met in the Fall of that year, the Whig members tried to break up the *new* Session by absenting themselves from voting to adjourn the old Session *sine die*, so that they could Constitutionally meet the next Wednesday morning; the State Constitution requiring the Legislature to meet "the first Monday in December next, ensuing the election of members." After the breaking up of the morning Session, the Sergeant-at-arms hunted up the delinquent Whigs, and at 3 o'clock there was a quorum obtained, and the doors locked. The Springfield *Register* of Dec. 11, 1840, mentions this matter, but thinks Uncle Abe " come off without damage, as it was noticed that his legs reached nearly from the window to the ground !"

A proposition was afterwards humorously proposed, to add another story to the new State House, so that fugacious members would have to go down the water spouts if they ran!

Tried for Scaring the Girls.

Thirty years ago, when Springfield was blooming into the dignity of its Capitalive position, the American House was its great hotel, (and it isn't its smallest yet,) and the resort of those who loved to spend a few hours in the society of the *bon vivants* who then assembled—Lincoln, Douglas, Shields, Ferguson, Herndon, (then a young man, but since the law partner of Uncle Abe,) and many others "not unknown to fame," could almost always be found here during the evening.

One evening as they were sitting in free converse in the bar-room, one of the chamber maids came in and informed the landlord that a man was under her bed.

It seems while stooping down to untie her gaiters, she saw a man under the bed. With rare presence of mind, she excused herself to her fellow servant as having forgotten some duty, and reported her discovery to the landlord. Boniface at once called for volunteers to secure the interloper. So eager were they for fun, that all volunteered. They surprised and captured the man, and brought him down to the bar-room; but what to do with him? was the next question. Springfield then had no vagabonds who made fees out of misfortunes—*i. c.* policemen—and

it was determined to treat him with the prompt justice peculiar to that era. A court was therefore got
together at once, all expectant of fun but the unfortunate culprit.

Judge Thomas Brown was decided upon to act as
Judge; Melborn, the talented, but eccentric State At-
torney, was detailed to prosecute; and Lincoln and
Douglas to defend the prisoner. Dr. Wallace acted
as Sheriff, and upon the jury were Dr. Merriman,*
Gen. Shields, John Calhoun (of Lecompton memory,)
Uri Manly, and many other well known personages.

Lawborn, though a regularly-educated and talented
lawyer, took occasion not only to be as "funny as he
could," but to imitate the prevailing style of oratory
too common in Illinois—a style in which the Hard-
shell-Baptist devil mingled with the rough dialect of
the back-woodsman.

"*May it please your Honor, and you, gentlemen of the
Jury:* The Legislature of Illinois, though it has legis-
lated upon every subject it could think of, has
omitted to pass any act against a man being born as
ugly as he pleases. If such an idea ever occurred to
my friend Lincoln here, when in the Legislature, I
know he would at once dismiss it, not only as too personal, but as repugnant to his honest heart. As for
myself, I like ugly men. An ugly man stands up on
his own merits. Nature has done nothing for him,
and he feels that he must labor to supply the deficit
by amiability and good conduct generally. There
is not an ugly man in this room but has felt this. A
pretty man, on the contrary, trusts his face to supply
head, heart and everything. He is an anomaly in

---

* Afterward murdered and robbed on the Pacific.

nature, as though the productions had been at fault as to sex, and sought to correct it when too late. "They are girl's first loves, and doting husband's jealous bane. I confess I don't like pretty men half so well as I do pretty women.

"No, gentlemen, ugliness is nothing. It is manners that is everything. The ugliest man that ever lived, never intentionally frightened a woman—nay, never was so unfortunate as to do so. But this creature, gentlemen of the Jury, this mendacious wretch whom you set in judgment upon—this creature, who would doubtless enter for a prize of beauty at a vanity fair—how has he failed in his duty to society? Why, gentlemen, by crawling under the bed upon which two fair damsels were about to expose their loveliness to Diana's envious gaze. Did he wish to woo them? Petruche's was rough in his wooing—this man was mean! Woman loves not surprises. Their hearts are fond of open sieges. This is the case of all women-kind. Maugre the slander of Hudibras:

> "He that woos a maid,
> Must lie, love, and flatter."

It is a *mystery* that adds to beauty, and the woman who surrenders that to importunity or surprise, has lost half her vantage ground. The story of Guyges and Candaules' queen, if not paralleled here, is not without its moral. What else meant this wretch, gentlemen of the Jury, but to surprise these charming damsels when only armed with the light shield that the Huntress and the cotton plant throws over earthly beauty? Or, perhaps he meant more—his own guilty heart can only accuse him there.

"Gentlemen of the Jury, the failure of our Legislature to provide a specific punishment for such miscreants, as this—lecherous creatures, who steal upon woman amid the mysteries of the bed-room—is no reason why society should fold its arms and leave woman's hidden beauties to be anatomized by guilty eyes. No, gentlemen of the Jury, outraged decency cries for its victim, and here he tremblingly, guiltily stands.

"Gentlemen of the Jury, where are the spirits of the fathers of the Constitution? Are they not hovering over us in the air of the still summer day? Are they not wailing upon the winds that sweep over our prairies? Are they not heard in the sigh of the mountain pine? Are they not abroad in all lands, whispering to earth's downtrodden millions like a voice of hope? Yes, gentlemen of the Jury! and where was this creature then? Why, creeping under the bed of two girls, hazzarding the chance of overturning—well, it matters not."

--And much more, in a view that needed to be heard to be appreciated.

Lincoln followed, illustrating with anecdotes meet for the place and occasion, of which I recollect only the opening. "Gentlemen of the Jury," said he, "the remarks of my friend Lawborn about ugly men, comes home to my bosom like the sweet oders of a rose to its neighboring great sister, the cabbage. It was a grateful, a just tribute to that neglected class of the community—ugly men.

"I wish to say something for my client, although it must in candor be admitted, that he had 'gone to pot.' I don't see why we should throw the kettle after him ; he may be the victim of circumstances ; he looks very bashful now, and it may be the girls scared him ; who knows? At least I claim for him the benefit of a doubt.

" Why, gentlemen, many of us have, or might have suffered from a concatenation of circumstances as strong as that under which my client labors. Let me relate a little personal anecdote in illustration. When I was making the secret canvass of this country, with my friend Cartwright, the Pioneer Preacher, we chanced to stop at the house of one of our old Kentucky farmers, whose log-cabin parlor, kitchen and hall were blended in one, and only separated at night by sundry blankets hung up between the beds. As we were candidates for the august Legislature of Illinois, our host treated us with the privacy of a blanket room. During the night I was awakened by some one throwing their leg over me with some force. I thought it was neighbor Cartright, and took hold of it to give it a toss back ; but it didn't feel like one of his white oak legs, and while I was feeling it to ascertain the correctness of my half-awake doubts, a stifled scream thoroughly awakened me, and the leg was withdrawn. Why, gentlemen, would you believe me ? It was the leg of our host's daughter! Imagine my position if you can ! What an *apparent* breach of hospitality ! While I was imagining an excuse for my conduct, the 'old folks' struck a light, and the blanket between our bed and that of the buxon damsel, was discovered to have been pulled down ! More damning proof, thoght I. I feigned sleep, but kept one corner of my left eye open for obseavation. The blanket was soon fixed up, and I was greatly relieved to hear the damsel explain to her mother that she herself had invaded our bed while dreaming, caused by some un-digestable vegetables she had eaten for her supper. Our host was serene and affable in the morning, and I had no need to apologize ; but, gentlemen, imagine what an escape I had, and have mercy on my client."

Uncle Abe made a side splitting speech all through, and Douglas followed with a " constitutional " argument.

The Jury returned a verdict of "guilty of scaring the girls," and the Judge sentenced the culprit to be whipped in the back yard, by the girls he had scared.

Dr. Wallace, the acting Sheriff, (no, a paymaster in the army,) went out and bought a cow hide, and the fellow was soon tied up to a post, and the girls made per force to give him thirty-nine well laid on.

The whole affair was a rich evening's divertisement, and cost nothing more than a few lost vest buttons and strained button holes.

It is needless to say that the fellow became a *non est* man from that day thenceforth.

"Thank God for the Sassengers."

Most of the readers of this have perhaps read a good story of Oliver Ditson, the celebrated Boston Music publisher. After he had been in business sev-eral years, his New Hampshire friends invited him to open his Thanksgiving in his native town, he ac-cepted the invitation and started with some of his friends. On the way Ditson was the great man of the occasion, and was therefore placed at the head of the table, when it devolved upon him to ask the blessing. Now Oliver practiced more religion than he knew the exact forms for, and he was in a sad dilemma; but he essayed boldly the task. He thanked God for all the 'creature comforts' there were upon the table— for all there ever had been—for all that was expected. But how to quit? He went on, thanking and trying to think at the same time how 'blessings' ended, but to no purpose. Knives rattled, plates moved, and Oliver saw the hungry people were getting impatient, and he came to the end in a real business like style, with—   " Yours, respectfully,

OLIVER DITSON."

Almost as good an anecdote is told by Uncle Abe of one of his old friends, a Mr. Sawyer, who merchandized either in Macon or Champaign County. Sawyer, was a Yankee, and distinguished for little besides an immoderate liking for " sassingers," as he called that "linked sweetness" which polite people call sausages. When Uncle Abe was stumping the Sangamon District for Congress, it befell that he and Sawyer met at the same country hotel, which was kept by a hardshell Baptist, whose foible was long prayers and blessings at table. They—Lincoln and Sawyer —happened to be going to the same town by the same coaches. So they were up betimes and ready, but breakfast was delayed. They at last got to the table, and the Deacon was just closing his eyes preliminary to the blessing, when the stage horn blew.

"Bless me, Deacon, there's the stage ready," cried

the Sawyer; "thank God for the sassengers, and let us fall too."

I hardly need say the Deacon's blessing—and perhaps his breakfast were spoiled. But Sawyer had his "sassengers."

Was'nt Murder After All.

When the present State House of Illinois, was being built—and it's a passable edifice, baring it is too low in the ground, and the *summer house* up on its top is too low to catch the cool breezes—it chanced that among the workmen engaged upon it was a New Yorker named Johnson. This man had a sovereign contempt for most of the shinplasters then circulating in Illinois; nor was he much amiss in this, for if it was now in existence, it would be exchangable at par with Jeff Davis' shinplasters. But through the instrumentality of Col. Thornton's negotiations in New York with McAlister of Stebbins, (a claim, by the way, that has never been settled but came near *settling* the State *a la* Mattoon,) a large amount of the bills of the New York *Metropolitan Bank* were put into circulation about Springfield. For this currency Johnson conceived so great a partiality that the passion of avarice soon turned it into a mania. He bought all these notes his means permitted, and stored them away about his person with miserly care.

One Sunday Johnson was invited to ride out to the Cut-off by a man (Smith for the nonce) and accepted. They did'nt stop at the Cut-off, but went direct to

Sangamon River. Here, they were overheard quarrelling.

Smith came home without Johnson, who was soon missed, and as he was known to have gone away with Smith, that individual was soon put in that log building still standing (it did in '62) back of Carrigan's Hotel, and which has since served as a hen house, etc. (Why don't Butler take a picture of it, to show the "rising generation what a small house used to hold all the *known* or *taken* rogues of old Sangamon?)

The examination of Smith, did not take place until the river bank had been examined. There were signs of a struggle on the bank, and to the water's edge, which gave force to the evidence of the man who heard them in dispute, and all felt convinced that Johnson had been murdered. Although a careful examination and dredging of the river failed to produce the body, Smith was committed for trial.

Uncle Abe was engaged as counsel for Johnson, but had little hopes of being of any earthly aid to him.

At last the day of trial came, and the prisoner plead "not guilty."

I think it was Melborn who was the prosecuting Attorney; before the prosecution had opened the case Uncle Abe rose and said:

"May it please the Court, I have a motion to make before the prosecution opens; and as it may save the Court some unnecessary labor, I hope it will be entertained. *I move that the indictment be quashed and the prisoner discharged!*"

The astonishment of the crowded Court room was immense, shared alike by Judge, bar and spectators. As soon as the Judge recovered his equanimity he asked:

" Upon what grounds is so extraordinary a motion made ?"

" Why the man Johnson, was not murdered at all, and I have the pleasure of introducing *him to the presence of the Court.*"

Johnson was led forward. Hundreds recognized him immediately. The excitement was so great that the Judge adjourned the Court.

It seems that the parties had quarreled, Johnson had been pushed into the river, but had got out and wandered off in a state of partial aberation of mind and had been working on a farm. His passion for Metropolitan Bank Notes and his name suggested an idea that he was the missing man, and he was opportunely produced in time to save a man from being hung.

Joe Reed's Mule Hunt.

One of the best natured fellows in the world, when he is not mad, is Joe Reed, of Logan County, Illinois, Joe is a staunch Republican—a real rip-rarer in the cause, and has given Uncle Abe the lift of a mighty broad pair of shoulders more than once, although at first he had a poor opinion of the rail-splitter. Thereby hangs a tale.

In 18—, (the date is forgotten on account of the coldness of the weather that winter,) Joe lost a couple of mules. After they had been gone for a long time, he chanced to hear of them in a settlement somewhere within the present bounds of Macon County, Illinois. At the first opportunity Joe started on a mule hunt, determined to find either the mules or some *trace* of them. On reaching the neighborhood in question, Joe was satisfied that an old fellow named Bosby Sheel, had his mules; and when he went in person, and saw them, the assurance of his eyes made "assurance double sure." He at once made claim, but the old fellow had heard that possession was nine points of the law—he declined to surrender them; Joe immediately appealed to old Squire P———, who at once summoned the holder of the mules to his Court. The Squire informed Joe that he would have to prove property; but Joe said he would only have to swear to his property. In this dilemma, the Squire adjourned Court till after dinner and remarked to Joe that he had better get a lawyer.

"There is young Abe Lincoln, he don't live far from here, and he'll be at my house after dinner."

As he was the only lawyer immediately thereabouts, Joe thought he had best employ him, in order to "have the law on his side."

Soon after dinner a stranger arrived, and the Justice (who was landlord of the only hotel in the settlement,) whispered to Joe, that that was the lawyer.

"What!" exclaimed Joe, "that lean, lank gawky? "Why, I'll bet both of them mules I know more law nor he does, for I'm a 'Squire at home myself—I am."

"But his looks is mighty deceivin', I tell you," said Boniface. "He's gin out to be one of the piertest young fellows short o' Sangamon."

But Joe was decided, and the 'Squire re-convened his Court, he having the meantime laid the case before his young friend, the lawyer, and got his opinion.

Acting his own lawyer, Joe felt it due to his course to give a concise statement of the law. As he stood up, he still continued to read from a green-covered book that had engaged his attention most of the day It was one of Cooper's latest novels. As Joe gave his version of the law, it seemed to 'Squire P—— that he was *reading* the law.

"Is that really the law?" said he, as Joe finished his version of the law—not the book. "Let me see that book."

Joe mechanically handed it to him.

After pouring over it for some time, he handed it back, with an air of disappointment, remarking:

"Drat me! if I see any sich law in that book."

"Well, it ain't no wonder ye don't—that's the *Red Rover*, a novel and not a law book, and you've been and lost my place too," Joe found his place, and continued: "what I told you is what the law says, and I know it's so."

"Well, as you're a 'Squire, too, I reckon you ought to know. As the mules don't belong to old man Bosby Sheel and you swear they are you'rn, I hold he's bound to give 'em up."

Joe rallied the old Squire rather hard about looking over the *Red Rover* for extra law, but finally "give a treat" and left the Squire and his friend in the best of humors.

———

Said Uncle Abe when he had the small-pox, "I now can give something to every one who calls."

Has no Influence with the Administration.

Judge Baldwin, an old and highly respectable and sedate gentleman, called a few days since on Gen. Halleck, and presuming upon a familiar acquaintance in California formerly, solicited a pass outside of our lines, to see a brother in Virginia, not thinking that he would be met with a refusal, as both his brother and himself were good Union men.

"We have been deceived too often," said General Halleck, "and I regret I can't grant it."

Judge B. then went to Stanton, and was very briefly disposed of with the same result. Finally he obtained an interview with Uncle Abe, and stated his case.

"Have you applied to Gen. Halleck?" inquired the President.

"And met with a flat refusal," said Judge B.

"Then you must see Stanton," continued Uncle Abe.

"I have, and with the same result," was the reply.

"Well, then," said Uncle Abe, with a smile of good humor, "I can do nothing; for you must know *that I have very little influence with this Administration.*

A Touching Incident.

The following incident, which occurred at the White House, will appeal to every heart. It reveals unmistakably the deep kindness of Uncle Abe's character:

"At a reception recently at the White House, many persons present noticed three little girls poorly dressed, the children of some mechanic or laboring man, who had followed the visitors into the house to gratify their curiosity. They were passed from room to room, and were passing through the reception room with some trepidation, when Uncle Abe, called to them : "Little girls, are you going to pass me without shaking hands?" Then he bent his tall, awkward form down, and shook each little girl warmly by the hand. Everybody in the apartment was spellbound by the incident, so simple in itself, yet revealing so much of Uncle Abe's character."

A Lincoln Man Ducked.

During the canvass between Uncle Abe, and Peter Cartright, the celebrated Pioneer Preacher, it chanced that Cartright, was returning to his home from the Williamsville and Wiggins Lane settlement. The nearest crossing of the Sangamon was at Carpenter's Mills, where there was the convenience of a ferry instead of a bridge, as is now the case. Upon the hill on the western side of the river, Cartright saw a man elevated upon a barrel in front of a little grocery— and on nearing him, he discovered that he was giving the Democrats in general, and Uncle Peter Cartright in particular, a perfect fusilade of small shots of slang and abuse.

"I tell you, boys, I'm a Whig,—a real Harrison Tippecanoe and Tyler too, Whig," said he. "I'm for putting down all these cuss'd locofocos, and if we can't vote 'em down, why I go for lickin' em' down. There's long Abe Lincoln that's runnin' for the Legislature—he's the chap to vote for. He's one of the people—split rails and got his edycation by moonlight. He don't go round the country prayin' and preachin' like that mean Methodist cuss, Peter Cartright, that's runnin' agin him. I'd like to know what we wants of a parson to make laws for us? Just elect him, and fust you know he'll have a bill into the Legislature, to fine us for not goin' to meetin' or for drinkin' a glass of whisky. I'll tell you what, if he ever comes round here, I'll just pass him inter the Sangamon—certain—sure."

Just here Uncle Peter Cartright enquired for the ferryman.

"I'm the ferry-*man*, old hoss," sung out the rustic orator, "and ken put ye cross the river in no time."

Uncle Peter signified his desire to cross, and the twain started towards the ferry boat. The Preacher stepping into the boat, hitched his horse to the side, while the ferryman shoved out into the stream.

"So you are a Lincoln man?" queried Uncle Peter.

"I'm that hoss."

"And so I presume you would douse a Cartright man if you had a chance?"

"I mought do it stranger."

"Certainly you would douse Mr. Cartright?"

"Sure's winkin', old fellow."

"Well Sir, I am Peter Cartright at your service," and before the ferryman recovered from his surprise Uncle Peter pitched him into the river, took the pole and put himself across the river.

The ferryman did'nt vote for Uncle Peter but he altered his opinion of Methodist preachers in general and Uncle Peter in particular.

A Comparison.

One day as Uncle Abe, and a friend were sitting on the House of Representatives steps, the session closed, and the members filed out in a body. Uncle Abe looked after them with a serious smile. "That reminds me," said he, "of a little incident when I was a boy; my flat boat lay up at Alton on the Mississippi, for a day, and I strolled about the town. I saw a large stone building, with massive stone walls, not so handsome though, as this, and while I was looking at it, the iron gateway opened, and a great body of men came out. "What do you call that?" I asked a by-stander. "That," said he, "is the State Prison, and those are all thieves going home. Their time is up."

"There's Enough for All."

Uncle Abe was terribly bored by the office seekers, even before the Presidential house-warming had scarcely began. The Illinois politicians were the most ravenous pap-Suckers of all.

"Just wait a little," said Uncle Abe, "I can assure you, as L——d S——t did the swine, 'there's enough for all.'"

"Let us have the story, Uncle Abe," said one of the crowd, who evidently expected something rich.

"Why, you see," began Uncle Abe, "I attended court many years ago at Mt. Pulaski, the first county seat of Logan County, and there was the jolliest set of rollicking young Lawyers there that you ever saw together. There was Bill F——n, Bill H——n, L——d S——t, and a lot more, and they mixed law and Latin, water and whisky, with equal success. It so fell out that the whisky seemed to be possessed of the very spirit of Jonah. At any rate, S——t went out to the hog-pen, and, leaning over, began to 'throw up Jonah.' The hogs evidently thought it feed time, for they rushed forward and began to squabble over the voided matter.

"'Don't fight (hic),' said S——t : 'there's enough (hic) for all.'"

—The politicians couldn't see anything to laugh at, although the "snubbin" was plain enough.

* * *

Making a President.

Uncle Abe, in elucidating his estimate of Presidential honors, tells a clever story, as he always does, when he sets about it. It seems that Windy Billy, who is a politician of no ordinary pretensions, was a candidate for the Consulship of Bayonne, and he urged his appointment with the eloquence of a Clay or a Seward. He boasted vociferously of his activity in promoting the success of the Republican ticket, and averred with his impassioned earnestness that he and he alone had made Uncle Abe President.

"Ah!" exclaimed Uncle Abe, "and it was you who made me President, was it?" a twinkle in his eye all the time.

"Yes," said Billy, rubbing his hands and throwing out his chest, as a baggage-master would a small valise, "yes, I think I may say I am the man who made you President."

"Well, Billy, my boy, if that's the case, it's a h–ll of a muss you got me into, that's all."

Uncle Abe Boss of the Cabinet.

A prominent Senator was remonstrating with Uncle Abe a few days ago about keeping Mr. Chase in his Cabinet, when it was as well known that Mr. C. is opposed, tooth and nail, to Uncle Abe's re-election.

"Now, see here," said Uncle Abe, "when I was elected I resolved to hire my four Presidential rivals, pay them their wages and be their "boss." These were Seward, Chase, Cameron and Bates ; but I got rid of Cameron after he had played himself out. As to discharging Chase or Seward, don't talk of it. I pay them their wages and am their boss, and would'nt let either of them out on the loose for the fee simple of the Almaden patent."

Uncle Peter Cartright's Wonder.

Some of the farmers in and about Sagamon county,

Illinois, have been and still are so intent on cattle-raising, that the business is a sort of cattle-mania. Uncle Peter was one Sunday preaching near a good old deacon of this sort, whose piety was somewhat like that of a cardplaying lady mentioned by Addison, (Spectator No. 7,) who had a set hour for her devotions, and if she happened to be at a game, would get a friend to " hold her hand " while she said her prayers. Our worthy deacon was rather vain of his "gift" praying and saying " blessings " at table. As a matter of courtesy, he might occasionally ask a visiting preacher to pray or ask a blessing ; but he never failed to exhibit his " gift " to his visitors. He had a sing-song way of " getting it off," at the same time beating time with his hands on either side of his plate. On the occasion alluded to, he began—

" Oh Lord ! (thump) bless the creature comforts (thump) provided for our (thump) sustenance (thump.) Bless it (thump) to our needs (thump) and necessities, (thump). Lead us aright, (thump) but if we stray (thump) put us back (thump) into the right path, (thump). Bless the stranger (thump) that comes beneath our roof, (thump) and keep his feet (thump) in pleasant paths, (thump). What we ask (thump) amiss, (thump) withhold ; (thump) but grant us what our (thump) short-sightedness omits, (thump) and thine be the glory (thump) now and for ever, (thump) a——."

And here the old deacon stopped suddenly, opened his eyes, and looking across the table, asked :

" Son John, did Mr. Jones settle yet for that Durham cow ?"

"Yes, father—it's all right."

"Amen," concluded the deacon.

"Cattle! cattle!" exclaimed Uncle Peter in ill-concealed disgust.

"Why, you can't say your prayers without having cattle running through your head; I wonder the Lord don't turn such christians into cattle!"

Uncle Abe a Shaksperian.

When Uncle Abe was making a plea in one of the county Circuit Courts, not far from Springfield, one of the lawyers becoming sensible that he was being out-generaled, remarked to Uncle Abe, as he sat down—

"I smell a mice."

"Why don't you quote Shakspeare correctly?" said Uncle Abe.

"Why," said the other, "I was not aware that I was quoting Shakspeare at all."

"Certainly you were, and had you done it properly, it would have been more expressive and less vulgar. The correct expression is, "I smell a device."

The Running Sickness.

In the Black Hawk war, Uncle Abe belonged to a militia company in the service. On a scout, the company encountered the Indians, and in a brisk skirmish drove them some miles, when, night coming on, our forces encamped. Great was the consternation on discovering that Lincoln was missing. His absence, or rather his stories, from the bivouac, was a misfortune. Suddenly, however, he came into camp. "Maj. Abe, is that you? Thought you were killed. Where've you been?" were the startling speculations. "Yes," said Uncle Abe, "this is me—ain't killed either." "But where have you been all the time?" "Oh, just over there." "But what were you over there for? Didn't run away, did you?" "No," said he deliberately, "I don't think I run away; but, after all, I reckon if anybody had seen me going, and had been told I was going for a doctor, he would have thought somebody was almighty sick."

How to Get Rid of Rats.

So thick had the rats become in Logan County, a few years ago, that the means of getting rid of the nuisance was freely discussed. The newly organized Agricultural Society, finally concluded to offer three premiums for the then largest numbers. The man who took the largest prize, exhibited over 1,700 scalps all caught in the space of three weeks. At the time these prizes were pending, Uncle Abe attended Court there, and Col. L——n, (a considerable gourmand,) by the way, was discussing the best way to get rid of the rats, and finally asked Uncle Abe's opinion.

"Why," said Uncle Abe, "rats are a 'cunning cattle,' and soon find out how things are going."

I introduce them to your table as a delicacy, and when they find out you are making 'game' of them they will soon give you a wide berth."

The Colonel winced under a faint impression ; but silently ratified Uncle Abe's conclusions. "Yes," chimed in M——, "we might go so far as to use their pelts to ornament our winter clothing."

A Palpable Application.

On a late occasion, when the White House was open to the public, a farmer from one of the border counties of Virginia told Uncle Abe that the Union soldiers, in passing his farm, had helped themselves not only to hay, but his horses, and he hoped the President would urge the proper officer to consider his claim immediately. "Why, my dear sir," replied Uncle Abe, blandly, "I couldn't think of such a thing. If I considered individual cases, I should find work for twenty Presidents!" Bowie urged his needs persistently ; Uncle Abe declined good-naturedly. "But," said the persevering sufferer, "couldn't you just give me a line to Colonel —— about it ? just one line ?" 'Ha, ha, ha!" responded amiable Uncle Abe, shaking himself fervently, and crossing his legs the other way, "that reminds me of old Jack Chase out in Illinois." At this the crowd huddled forward to listen. "You have seen Jack—I knew him like a brother—used to be a lumberman on the Illinois, and he was steady and sober, and the best raftsman on the river. It was quite a trick twenty-five years ago to take the logs over the rapids, but he was skillful with a raft, and always kept her straight in the channel. Finally a steamboat was put on, and Jack—he's dead now, poor fellow!—was made captain of her. He used to take the wheel going through the rapids. One day, when the boat was plunging and wallowing along the boiling current, and Jack's utmost vigilance was exercised to keep her in the narrow channel. a boy pulled his coat tail, and hailed him with, 'Say, Mister Captain! I wish you'd just stop your boat a minute—I've lost my apple overboard!' "

Uncle Abe on the Whisky Question.

A committee, just previous to the fall of Vicksburg, solicitous for the *morale* of our armies, took it upon themselves to visit the President and urge the removal of General Grant.

"What for?" asked Uncle Abe.

"Why," replied the busy-bodies, "he drinks too much whisky."

"Ah!" rejoined Uncle Abe, "can you inform me gentlemen, where General Grant procures his whisky?"

The committee confessed they could not.

"Because," added Uncle Abe, with a merry twinkle in his eye, "If I can find out, I'll send a barrel of it to every General in the field!"

The delegation retired in reasonable good order.

Edwards vs. Lincoln.

One day soon after Uncle Abe began the canvass with Judge Douglas for the United States Senate Lincoln, Editor, accosted Nivian W. Edwards, (Uncle Abe's brother-in-law,) as Mr. Lincoln himself.

"Well," said Edwards, "I think I must be growing taller and uglier every day, for this is the sixth time I've been taken for Abe within a week."

Notwithstanding Edwards was a Democrat and a joker, Uncle Abe made him a commissary in the army.

Metalic Ring.

The new practical postal currency have upon the face, a faint oval ring of bronze, encircling the vignette. Uncle Abe being asked its use, replied that it was a faint attempt on the part of Mr. Chase, to give the new currency a metalic ring.

A Grateful Postmaster.

Said a long legged hoosier, on receiving the appointment of Postmaster, in Sangamon County, "I tell you Uncle Abe, you're a hoss," " yes replied Uncle Abe, a *draft* horse."

A Serious Joke.

WASHINGTON, Eebruary 18, 1864.

To WM. FISHBACK :—

When I fixed a *plan* for an election in Arkansas I did it in ignorance that your convention was at the same work. Since I learned the latter fact I have been constantly trying to yield my *plan* to theirs. I have sent two letters to General Steel, and three or four dispatches to you and others, saying that (General Steel,) must be master, but that it will probably be best for him to keep the convention on its own *plan.* Some single mind must be master, else there will be no agreement on any thing; and General Steel, commanding the military, and being on the ground, is the best man to be that master. Even now citizens are telegraphing me to postpone the election to a later day than either fixed by the Convention or me This discord must be silenced.

A LINCOLN.

A young Massachusetts soldier, named Merrill. writes a Washington correspondent, had on ounce ball pass through his head during the battle of Fredericksburg. It entered near his right eye and was extracted behind his left ear. Another ball would have entered a vital part of his body had it not been arrested by a Testament, in which it lodged. When this safeguard was shown to Uncle Abe, he sent to the hospital a handsome pocket Bible, in which was written: "Charles V. Merrill, Co. A. 19th Massachusetts, from A. Lincoln."

"MAJOR-GENERAL GRANT,—Understanding that your lodgment at Chattanooga and Knoxville is now secure I wish to tender you, and all under your command, my more than thanks—my profoundest gratitude—for the skill, courage, and perseverence with which you and they, over so great difficulties, have effected that important object. God bless you all!

A. LINCOLN."

Fix the Date.

Uncle Abe, was conversing with some friends and remarked, "There's a good Time coming," a country-man stepped up to Uncle Abe, and said: "Mister, you could'nt fix to date, could yous?"

Rival of Uncle Abe.

Old Abe has got off many good things since he left Springfield, but the following equals anything which has proceded from that veteran joker.

"In the Georgia Legislature, Mr. Linton Stephens, brother of the rebel Vice President, introduced a resolution in the House of Representatives declaring that peace be officially offered to the enemy after every Confederate victory."

"There I am, and here is Mrs. Lincoln."

Uncle Abe's Estimate of the Senate.

Uncle Abe, says that in the Senate, he "owns nine of the Senators and one-half of another." "Who owns the other half?" asked a gentleman to whom Uncle Abe was speaking. "Henry Wilson of Massachusetts," replied the Chief Magistrate, "Wilson is for me," says the President, "before breakfast; rather against me while his digestion is going on after it; loves me like pie during the hours which he spends visiting the various departments and asking for places and patronage; and bitterly my enemy from seven every evening until he goes to bed, drops asleep and commences snoring. Wilson is carrying water on both shoulders but I guess he'll get a wetting and soil his clothes before he gets through."

"Thought he Must be Good for Something."

An Illinois man who had known the "boy Mayor," John Hay, from boyhood, was expressing to Uncle Abe, after the massacre at Olustee, some regret that he should have supposed him capable of any military position.

"About Hay," said Uncle Abe, "the fact was, I was pretty much like Jim Hawks, out in Illinois, who sold a dog to a hunting neighbor, as a first-rate coon dog. A few days after, the fellow brought him back, saying he 'wasn't worth a cuss for coons.' 'Well,' said Jim, 'I tried him for everything else, and he wasn't worth a d——n, and so I thought he *must* be good for coons.'"

Aptly Said.

To a man who was condoling Uncle Abe on the disaster at Olustee, and suggesting how it might have been prevented, he said :

"Your remarks are well intended, doubtless ; but they do little less than aggravate a thing which I can't help thinking might have been helped. It reminds me of a story that I read when I was a boy. An old fellow who had clambered rather high into an apple tree, fell and broke his arm. A sympathizing and philosophic neighbor, seeing his mishap, went to his aid. 'Ah,' said he, 'if you had followed my plan you would have escaped this.' 'Indeed, what is your plan?' enquired the groaning man. 'Why, never to let go both hands, till you get one hold somewhere else.'"

The would-be Brigadier saw the point, and left.

"I see you've got to the sticking point at last," as the Democrat remarked to a slippery Republican, whose team had gone into the ground up to the hub.

"They have gone up every Creek and Bayou where it was a little damp."

"Linkums" Sold Cheap.

During the Presidential contest of 1860, there was
an Italian artist of plaster figures in Springfield, who
supplied "leetel Linkums," as he called his figures,
faster than ever Uncle Abe did. He succeeded in
putting one of these Republican penates into every
Republican house in town, but they finally became a
"drug" in the market. However, he kept his "asking
price" up ; but his selling price was as various as his
buyers, and hard to deal with.

One day, with a load of these upon his head, he entered a jeweller's shop, and accosted the man behind
the counter with—

"You buys 'em leetel Linkums?"

"No—don't want 'em."

"Sells 'em cheap," persisted the Italian.

"Well, how do you sell to-day?"

"Fifty cent piece."

"I'll give you a dollar for the lot," said A——, expecting to pose the Italian.

"You takes 'em," greedily exclaimed the artist, and
he left Mr. L. A. A——n with a lot of plaster on hand
which he had hard work to give away.

———

"There's an odor of nationality about those bills,"
said Secretary Chase, showing a lot of the firstlings
of his greenbacks to Uncle Abe.

"A very good figure of speech," replied Uncle Abe,

"but you must not get too many under the public nostril, or your figure of speech will be an odor of fact."

April 1, 1862, greenbacks, 100. April 1, 1864, greenbacks, 55.

Uncle Abe as a Pilot.

The captain of one of the Mississippi river steamers one morning, while his boat was lying at her moorings at New Orleans, waiting for the tardy pilot, who, it appears, was a rather uncertain sort of fellow, saw a tall, gaunt Sucker make his appearance before the captain's office, and sing out—

"Hello, cap'n! you don't want a pilot nor nothin' about this 'ere craft, do ye?"

"How do you know I don't?" responded the captain.

"Oh, you don't understand; I axed you s'posin' you did?"

"Then, supposing I do, what of it?"

"Well," said Uncle Abe, for it was he, "I reckon I know suthin' about that ere sort o' business, provided you wanted a feller of jest about my size."

The captain gave him a scrutinising glance, and with an expression of countenance which seemed to say, "I should pity the steamer that you piloted,' asked—

"Are you acquainted with the river, and do you know where the snags are?"

"Well, ye-as," responded Uncle Abe rather hesitatingly, "I'm pretty well acquainted with the river, but the snags, I don't know exactly so much about them."

"Don't know about the snags?" exclaimed the captain, contemptuously, "don't know about the snags! You'd make a pretty pilot!

At this Uncle Abe's countenance assumed anything but an angelic expression, and with a darkened brow and a fiercely flashing eye, he drew himself up to his full height, and indignantly roared back in a voice of thunder:

"What do I want to know where the snags are for, old sea-hoss? I know where they ain't, and there's where I do my sailing!"

It is sufficient to know that Uncle Abe was promptly engaged, and that the captain takes pleasure in saying that he proved himself one of the best pilots on the river.

(Wonder if Uncle Abe has forgotten how to sail in clear water?   A. A.)

Uncle Abe's Valentine.

Uncle Abe on the 14th of last February, received a valentine in the shape of a picture of the American eagle, with a financial allusion. The bird of freedom appeared to be engaged in picking up gold coin, while at the end of the bird most remote from his head there was a pile of "green-backs," into which this coin seemed to have been mysteriously transmuted.

Uncle Abe, who takes such things philosophically, and always acknowledges a palpable hit with grace and good natured cheerfulness, went to his Secretary of the Treasury, to exhibit his bird, in order that the latter might enjoy the joke with him. Mr. Chase, however, was not disposed to take the matter in the same spirit Uncle Abe did ; but appeared to be much out of humor at this hieroglyphical attack upon his department of the government. In tones in which there was evidently a slight admixture of irritability, he remarked to Uncle Abe that he would like to know who had made this unwarrantable attack upon his financial management of the affairs of the nation—that he feared that some of his subordinates had got up this libel upon him, and that he would give a hundred dollars to know who had done it. Uncle Abe, whose question-asking proclivities are well known, said that the offer seemed liberal ; " but, Mr. Chase," said he, " before I shall make up my mind on this subject, will you allow me to ask you one question ?' " Certainly," replied the Secretary. "I merely wanted to understand," said Uncle Abe, " at which end of the bird you propose to pay ?" " '*Et tu Brute ?*' responded the head of the Treasury department. " If I am thus to be made the subject of ridicule, I must renew my application to be relieved from my duties as Secretary." " O, never mind ! never mind ! Mr. Secretary," said Uncle Abe, " we can soon remedy all these difficulties. All we have to do, after we have suppressed this rebellion, is to turn the bird end for end, and let the gold and 'greenbacks' remain just as they are and all will come out right." The Secretary, restored to good humor, agreed not to resign unless Seward did.

" That reminds me of a little story."

" My Mary Ann."

Many months ago the post commander at Cairo was a certain West Point colonel of a Northwestern regiment, noted for his soldierly qualities and rigid discipline.   One day he passed by the barracks and heard a group of soldiers singing the well-known street piece, "My Mary Ann."   An angry shade crossed his brow, and he forthwith ordered the men to be placed in the guard-house, where they remained all night The next morning he visited them, when one ventured to ask the cause of their confinement.

"Cause enough," said the rigid colonel; "you were singing a song in derision of Mrs. Colonel B——."

The men replied by roars of laughter, and it was some time before the choler of the Colonel could be sufficiently subdued to understand that the song was an old one, and sung by half the school-boys in the land, or the risibles of the men be calmed down to learn that the colonel's wife rejoiced in the name of " Mary Ann."

Uncle Abe made the Colonel a Brigadier the moment he heard this story.

Uncle Abe's Honor.

At one time Uncle Abe aspired to a position on the bench, and Mrs. Lincoln, so as to be prepared for the event, practiced the habit of calling her husband " his

Honor," or "your Honor," as the case might be.
Uncle Abe never, however, succeeded to the dignity
of the ermine ; but attending Circuit at Chicago, and
stopping at the ———— Hotel, Mrs. L. accompanied
her husband, as was her custom. Uncle Abe had
donned a bran new pair of boots, which were anything
but comfortable, and almost as uncertain as a pair of
skates to a learner on the keenest of ice. Mrs. Lincoln was enjoying herself in the parlor in a chit-chat
with a number of other ladies, and putting on as
many airs as her provincial position in Springfield
would admit, when a strange, rumbling sound dis-
turbed the pleasant company, who rushed out to learn
what was the matter. Lo and behold ! there was
Uncle Abe in the undignified predicament of tumb-
ling down stairs and bumping the end of his spine
upon every step. The new boots, or the swig of forty-
rod which he had taken in his bed-room, had proved
traitor to him. Mrs. Lincoln was nearly non-plussed,
but exclaimed in a consoling voice, "Is your Honor
hurt ?"

"No," said Uncle Abe, sitting gracefully on the
carpet, with legs spread out amidst the bevy of tit-
tering damsels, and rubbing the seat of his trowsers,
"No, my honor is not hurt but my—my—my head
is !"

"Smoke That."

During the session of the Legislature of Illinois, in
1836-7, the Sangamon County delegation of nine
members, became known as the "Long Nine," from

the fact of their remarkable average height. In this delegation were Uncle Abe, Gen. Baker, (killed at Bull's Bluff,) N. W. Edwards, (brother-in-law of Uncle Abe, and now Captain commissary,) and some others of note in their day. A law had passed the previous session to remove the capital from Vandalia to Springfield, to be carried out as soon as a new capitol could be built. In the meantime, Gen. W. L. D. Ewing, an influential Egyptian member, made periodical efforts to repeal the law and keep the capital at Vandalia. During the session of 1837, we had a regular tilt with the "long nine," during which, whenever Uncle Abe or Gen. Baker made a point, Ewing would be saluted with the cry "smoke that!" in allusion to "long nines," a popular kind of cigars used at that day. This probably gave rise to saying, " put that in your pipe and smoke it."

A Sufficient Reason.

Some one recently asked Uncle Abe why he didn't promote merit? "Because merit never helped promote me," said our Uncle Abe.

The Boy and the Bear.

A committee of the enemies of Mr. Chase called on the President just after the Pomroy circular was sent forth and advised him to purify his cabinet and let

Chase go. Old Abe replied that "it is not so easy a thing to let Chase go. I am situated very much as the boy was who held the bear by the hind legs. I will tell you how it was. There was a very vicious bear which, after being some time chased by a couple of boys, turned upon his pursuers. The boldest of the two ran up and caught the bear by the hind legs, while the other climbed up into a little tree, and complacently witnessed the conflict going on beneath, between the bear and his companion. The tussel was a sharp one, and the boy, after becoming quite exhausted, cried out in alarm, 'Bill, for God's sake come down and help me let this darned bear go!' Now, gentlemen," said Mr. Lincoln, "you see what a fix I am in—it may be dangerous to hold on to Chase, but it will require more assistance than I see at present, to help me let him go."

Too Deep.

During the Black Hawk war, when the valiant Illinoisians were in hasty retreat from what they thought certain scalping, and the roads exclusively' bad, in fact, unfathomable mud.—In this predicament, the corps in which Uncle Abe was, became somewhat scattered, when the officer commanding, called out to the men to form *two deep*. "Blast me!" shouted Abe from a slough, in which he was nearly buried, I am too deep already; I am up to the neck.'

'It's easier to pay when you've the money, than when you have'nt."

Uncle Abe's First Speech.

When Uncle Abe first made his appearance in the Illinois House of Representatives, and was desirous of delivering his sentiments on a certain measure, he rose and began :—" Mr. SPEAKER, *I conceive* ——" but could go no further. Thrice he repeated unsuccessfully the same attempt ; when Douglas, who had more confidence, and had been a year longer in the House, completely dumbfounded Abe by saying : " Mr. SPEAKER, The honorable gentleman has *conceived three times, and brought forth nothing.*

Cute.

One night Uncle Abe came wet and cold to a cross road tavern in Indiana, and found the fire more thoroughly blockaded with Hoosiers than mother Welles has been able to blockade the Southern Confederacy. Abe ordered the landlord to carry his horse a peck of catfish. " He can't eat catfish," said Boniface. "Try him," said Abe, " there's nothing like trying." The crowd all rushed after the landlord to see Abe's horse eat the peck of catfish. "He won't eat them, as I told you," said the landlord, on returning. " Then," coolly responded Uncle Abe, who had squatted on the best seat, " bring them to me and I'll eat them myself."

Abe's Spelling.

Being asked by a client in Springfield why he spelled so badly in his law papers, Uncle Abe replied, "Because, the Suckers are so cussed mean they won't pay for good spelling."

A Soldier's Theory of the War.

The soldiers at Helena, in Arkansas, used to amu se the inhabitants of that place, on their first arrival, by telling them yarns, of which the following is a sample :

"Some time ago Jeff. Davis got tired of the war and invited President Lincoln to meet him on neutral ground to discuss terms of peace. They met accordingly, and after a talk, concluded to settle the war by dividing the territory and stopping the fighting. The North took the Northern States, and the South the Gulf and seaboard Southern States. Lincoln took Texas and Missouri, and Davis Kentucky and Tennessee ; so that all were parcelled off excepting Arkansas. Lincoln did'nt want it—Jeff. would'nt have it. Neither would consent to take it, and on that they split ; and the war has been going on ever since."

Nigger Mathematics.

Uncle Abe was lately visited by one of the "On to

Richmond " sword of Gideon gentry, who confidently expressed the hope, so common among the Abolition noodles, that Lee's army would be " bagged." Uncle Abe grinned to the utmost of his classic mouth, and remarked that he was afraid there would be too much " nigger mathematics " in it. The visitor smiled at the allusion, as he felt bound in politeness to do supposing there must be something in it, though he could not see the point. " But I suppose you don't know what " nigger mathematics' is," continued Uncle Abe. " Lay down your hat a minute, and I'll tel, you." He, himself, resumed the sitting posture leaned back in his chair, elevated his heels on the table, and went on with his story. " There was a darkey in my neighborhood, called Pompey, who, from a certain quickness in figuring up the prices of chickens and vegetables, got the reputation of being a mathematical genius.

Johnson, a darkey preacher, heard of Pompey, and called to see him. ' Here ye're a great mat'm'tishum, Pompey.' ' Yes sar, you jas try.' ' Well Pompey, Ize compound a problem in mat'matics.' ' All right, sar.' ' Now, Pompey, spose dere am tree pigeons sittin' on a rail fence, and you fire a gun at 'em and shoot one, how many's left? ' ' Two, ob cooors,' replies Pompey after a little wool scratching. ' Ya-ya-ya,' laughs Mr. Johnson ; ' I knowed you was a fool, Pompey ; dere's *none* left—one's dead, and d'udder two's flown away.' " That's what makes me say," continued Uncle Abe, " that I am afraid there was too much nigger mathematics in the Pennsylvania campaign." And the result showed that in this instance, at least, the anecdote suited the fact. Lee's

army was then three pigeons.   One of them was taken
down at Gettysburg, but the other two flew off over
the Potomac.

Long and Short of it.

"Here I am, and here is Mrs. Lincoln, and thats
the long and short of it."—*Speech of Mr. Lincoln from
the balcony of the White House at Washington.*

A Handy Faculty.

Whilst Uncle Abe was passing, in his flat-boat, a
small town on the Wabash, an old chum accosted him
rom shore thus :—
  " Uncle Abe, are you asleep ?"
  " Why ?"
  " Because, I want to borrow some whiskey."
  " Then " said Abe, " *I am asleep.*"
And he rolled over drowsily on the flat-boat, and it
passed on.

Uncle Abe on Time.

A Methodist dominie was lecturing Abe on his love
of gambling.   " Ah Abraham, it is a grievous sin —in
the first place, consider the loss of time."   " Yes,'
replied Uncle Abe, " I have often begrudged the loss
of time—in *shuffling* and *dealing.*"

A Story that had no Reminder.

During a conversation which took place between Uncle Abe and a distinguished western senator, the recent legislative nominations for the next presidency were incidentally referred to. "Yes," said Uncle Abe, nursing his leg with evident gratification—" yes, senator, the current seems to be setting all one way!" "It does, really, seem to be setting all one way," was the answer of the senator ; "but, Mr. Lincoln, as you have told me several good stories since I have been here, permit me if you please, to tell *you* one. It has always been observed that the Atlantic Ocean, at the Straits of Gibraltar, constantly pours into the Mediterranean with tremendous volume. The Bosphorus empties into it, at its other end, and rivers are seen contributing to its waters all along its coast. It was for many years the constant puzzle of geographers, why the Mediterranean, under all these accessions, never got full, and overran its banks. After a while, however, a curious fellow took the notion of dropping a plummet in the center of the Straits, when, lo ! he discovered that, though the tremendous body of water on the surface was rushing inward from the ocean, a still more powerful body was passing outward, in a counter current, some twenty feet below !" "Oh, ah !" said Uncle Abe, seriously, evidently nonplussed, for the first time in his life ; "that *does not* remind me of any story I ever heard before !"

Has it "Gin Out?"

We do not know what joke Uncle Abe made when

he heard the news of the surrender of Plymouth. In regard to the Fort Pillow affair he made a Bunsby speech, but no joke. His last joke, of which we have any knowledge, occurred when Secretary Chase was starting on his trip to New York. Uncle Abe is like Cromwell without his military genius, and is very fond of playing practical jokes on his associates. It is said that after Cromwell had signed the warrant for the execution of King Charles he turned round to one of his colleagues and smeared his face with the ink. This he thought capital fun. Uncle Abe's jokes are of about the same quality. When Chase called upon him to say good bye, the Secretary of the Treas. ury asked for some information about the probable end of the war, saying it would help him greatly in getting more money in Wall street. "Do you want more money?" asked Lincoln, and then quickly added, "What! has the printing machine gin out?" This joke is fully equal to Cromwell's.

A Major.

At one of Uncle Abe's levees recently, among the Company was a Pennsylvania Avenue tailor whom Abe recognized but could not name. "My dear Sir, I remember your face, but I forget your name," said Uncle Abe. The knight of the needle whispered confidentially into Uncle Abe's ear. "I made your breeches." Uncle Abe took him most affectionately by the hand and exclaimed enthusiastically "Major Breeches, I am happy to meet you at the White House!"

A Dry Drop.

A refugee from Richmond was telling Uncle Abe of the sad state of affairs reigning there. Among other things he said liquor was so scarce that the rebel President himself could scarcely get a drop to drink.

"He ought not to have a drop *to drink* in this world or the next," said Uncle Abe.

"You are rather severe," replied the refugee.

"Well," said Uncle Abe, "if you think a drop would do him good, let it be a drop from the scaffold.'

Uncle Abe as a Physiognomist.

While the western governors were in conversation the other day, one of them asked him if he remembered a certain Major of the ———— Illinois regiment Uncle Abe replied that "he could'nt say that he did.'' The gentleman who addressed him then tried to jog the executive memory a little by mentioning a circumstance or two connected with the Major's history. Finally Uncle Abe remembered him very well—which fact he stated in the following graphic language: "O yes, I know who you mean. *It's that turkey egg faced fellow that you'd think did'nt know as much as a last year's bird's nest.*" This was the very individual referred to. It will be seen that Uncle Abe has other fortes than statesmanship—and that of a physiognoist mis one of them.

The Concrete vs. the Abstract.

Dick Yates, the jolly Governor of the Suckers, tells that he called on Uncle Abe one morning when he was trying to get the 88,000 "Hundredazers" accepted, and that during their interview Uncle Abe remarked: "Yates, I'll tell you the difference between the concrete and the abstract. When the Senate passed a resolution requesting me not to appoint any more Brigadiers, as the vacancies were all full, that's the concrete. But when a Senator comes up here with a long petition and a longer face, requesting me to make a brigadier out of some scallawag of a friend of his, as it happens every day—I call that the abstract."

Symptoms of Civilization.

Uncle Abe and his chums were wrecked and swamped once on a trip to New Orleans, and having waded ashore, were in search of shelter and refreshment, without much prospect of success, in a thickly timbered bottom. They had traveled through the forest a long distance, and were in despair of finding any human habitation, when they discovered a negro hanging on the projecting limb of a tree. "The joy," said Abe, when telling the adventure, "which this cheering view excited, cannot be described, for it convinced us that we were in a *civilized country.*"

Uncle Abe goes into Partnership.

In the days when Uncle Abe plied the flat-boat business on the Wabash and Sangamon, he made it a practice to troll for catfish and dispose of them to the planters in Mississippi, when passing their plantations. This brought him quite a revenue, which was always expended for "forty rod" whisky, or the fish were traded off direct for that fluid chain lightning. Once while passing the plantation of Mr. Percy, he was bound to have some forty rod, and went ashore with a fine lot of fish. A large party were assembled at the mansion of the aristocratic Percy; when Julius Cæsar informed him that Uncle Abe was below with some very fine fish. "Well," said Percy, "give him his forty rod as usual, and let him go." "But sah, he won't take it dis time," said the darkey, "he wants a hundred lashes on the bare back, well laid on massa." Uncle Abe insisted to the surprise of every one on this strange price for his fish, and Mr. Percy to humor him, complied, directing the overseer to cut him gently. When Uncle Abe had received the fiftieth lash, he cried, "Hold! I have got a partner in this business, to whom I have engaged to give half of whatever I should get for the fish—this overseer would not admit me only on that condition." O course the overseer had his share well paid, and Abe got his forty-rod as usual, with something added.

Abe Passing Counterfeit Money.

One day a poor woman ran into Uncle Abe's law office in great fright exclaiming :—

"Oh, Mr. Lincoln, my boy has swallowed a penny!"

"Was it a counterfeit," coolly asked Mr. Lincoln.

"No, certainly not," replied the woman, somewha indignantly.

"Oh! well, then *it will pass*, of course," said Uncle Abe.

It is hardly necessary to add that the anxious mother went home comforted and that the boy who "swallowed the penny," at the last Presidentia-election voted for "Honest Old Abe."

The Wrong Man Poulticed.

At the famous watering place, of the Blue Lick Springs, Uncle Abe was severely afflicted with a paitl n the stomach, which neither gin cock-tails nor otheer cordials could remove. It was night and he was in bed. His loving wife, unwilling to awake the domess tics, descended to the kitchen, and prepared -. mustard poultice, which she spread on her own handa kerchief, and proceeded with it to the distressed Uncle Abe. Before leaving him, she left a light dimly burning in the apartment; but deeply impressed with anxiety, she was not as careful as she might hav been in noting the number of her room.

Guided by a light which she saw shining in a chamber, and which she supposed was the one she had left, she entered, and gently raising the bed clothes, &c., laid the warm poultice upon a stomach but not the stomach of Uncle Abe.

"Hello there! What the——are you about?" shouted a voice of thunder, and the body and sleeves, whence it issued, sprang out of bed.

The lady screamed and ran; Uncle Abe rushed to the rescue from the next room, the waiters joined and a small scene ensued, much to the amusement of all concerned. The poulticed gentleman had indiscreetly left a light in his room, and this lured the lady from her path.

Uncle Abe was so amused and excited by the mistake that he quite forgot his pains; but early the next morning, with his wife and trunks, left for Springfield, Ill. The poulticed man still retains the handkerchief—a beautiful cambric—with the lady's name on it, the initials of Frances Amelia R. Todd.

Uncle Abe as School Superintendent.

When Uncle Abe kept grocery on the Sangamon he was elected as School Superintendent out of his district. It was his duty to examine the applicant teachers on mathematics; which he once did in this wise in his grocery store. "If two pigs weigh twenty pounds how much will a large hog weigh."

"Jump into the scales," said the weilder of the birch "and I'll soon tell you."

Abe did not examine him further in mathematics.

Uncle Abe's Nose.

Uncle Abe being asked once why he walked so crookedly? said, "Oh my nose, you see, is crooked, and I have to follow it!"

Take Away the Fowls.

After Uncle Abe had studied law some time and whilst travelling in the Prairie country in Knox County, Illinois, he stopped at the house of Mrs. Galt, an old Scotch lady whose husband was largely engaged in wool growing. Abe at this time was beginning to be proud of his learning, especially of his pronunciation of English. Mrs. Galt when dinner was over desired the servant in waiting to take away the fowls, which she, (as is sometimes done in Scotland), pronounced *fools*, "I presume, madam, you mean fowls" said Abe rather sententiously. "Very well, be it so," said Mrs. Galt; take away the *fowls*, but let the *fool* remain!"

Uncle Abe Well Fed.

Old Whitey, Abe's school master, said to him angrily one day, "Abraham you are better fed than taught!" "Should think I was," said Abe, "as I feed myself and you teach me!"

UNCLE ABE says there is a good deal of the devil in the Rebels. They sometimes fight like him, frequently run like him, and always lie like him.

A Man of Means.

Uncle Abe was asked by a client whether his neighbor Brown was "a man of means." "Well I reckon he ought to be," said Abe, "for he is just the meanest man in Springfield."

Call Again.

When Uncle Abe was taken sick recently, and Mrs Lincoln had sent for the doctor; Uncle Abe, having an aversion to physic, said, he had better call another time, as he was too sick then to joke with him.

Uncle Abe Swapped when a Baby.

Abe when asked whether he could account for his excessive homeliness said "when I was two months old I was the handsomest child in Kentuck, but my nigger nurse swapped me off for another boy just to please a friend who was going down the river whose child was rather plain looking."

Hit at Antietam.

Another story of Uncle Abe, too good to be lost, has leaked out. It seems he had accompanied a young lady to one of the hospitals in the capitol where the sympathizing creature, as in duty bound became interested in a wounded soldier. To all her inquiries as to the location of the wound, however, she could only get one reply, thus : "My good fellow where were you hit!" "At Antietam." "Yes, but where did the bullet strike you?" "At Antietam." "But where did it hit you !" "At Antietam." Becoming discouraged, she deputized Uncle Abe to prosecute the inquiry, which he did successfully Upon his rejoining her, she was more curious than. ever, when the President, taking both her hands in his said in his most impressive style. "My dear girl, the ball that hit *him*, would not have injured *you*. .

A Poor Crop.

An old acquaintance of Uncle Abe's called upon him a short time since with the view to getting hold of a contract. Uncle Abe told him that contracts were not what they were in Cameron's time. "In fact, said he, "they remind me now of a piece of meadow land on the Sangamon bottoms during a drouth" "How was that?" said the Sucker—"Why," said Abe, looking rather quizical, "the grass was so short that they had to lather before they could mow it."

Handy in Case of Emergencies.

During the fall of 1863, Uncle Abe was riding on the Virginia side of the Potomac, between Arlington Hights and Alexandria, accompanied by Dr. N——— of New Jersey. Passing the huge earth-work fortifications, the Doctor observed : " Mr. President, I have never yet been enabled to discover the utility of constructing and maintaining those forts. What is your opinion about them ?"

" Well doctor," replied Uncle Abe, " you are a medical man ! and I will ask you a question in the line of your profession. Can you tell me the use of a man's nipples ?" " No I can't " said the doctor " Well I can tell you," said Uncle Abe,—" They would be mighty handy if he happened to have a child."

Value of a Reputation.

A client of Uncle Abe's was tried for stealing, in Springfield, Illinois, when it was satisfactorily proven that he had acknowledged the theft to several persons. Uncle Abe argued in behalf of his client that he was such an abominable liar that no one could believe him and the jury ought not to. The judge charged against the prisoner, but to his astonishment the jury brought in a verdict that the accused was entirely unworthy of belief ; and he was therefore acquitted.

Didn't Like the Name.

A young U. S. Officer being indicted at Chicago, for an assault on an aged gentleman, Uncle Abe began to open the case thus: "this is an indictment against a soldier for assaulting an old man." "Sir," indignantly interrupted the defendant, "I am no soldier, I am an officer!" "I beg your pardon," said Abe, grinning blandly; "then, gentlemen of the jury, this is an indictment against *an officer*, who is *no soldier*, for assaulting an old man.

Uncle Abe's Good Bye.

When Uncle Abe joined the Sangamon Militia and entered on the Black Hawk war campaign, his Colonel was a small snipe of a fellow about four feet three inches. Physically, of course, Uncle Abe looked down upon his Colonel. Abe had rather a slouching look and gait at that time, and attracted by his awkward appearance, the dapper little Colonel thus saluted the future Executive and manufacturer of both Colonels and Brigadiers. "Come, Uncle Abe, hold up your head; higher, fellow!" "Yes sir." "Higher, fellow—higher." Abe stretched his lank neck to its greatest altitudinous tension and said, "What—so, Sir?" "Yes, fellow, a little higher." "And am I always to remain so?" "Yes, fellow, certainly!" "Then," said Uncle Abe, with a woeful countenance, "good bye, Colonel, for I shall never see *you again!*"

Uncle Abe's Last.

Yesterday a Western correspondent, in search for something definite in relation to the fighting now going on, stepped into the White House and asked the President if he had anything authentic from Gen. Grant. The President stated that he had not, as Grant was like the man that climbed the pole and then pulled the pole up after him.— *Washington Union, May* 16.

CONTENTS.

www.ingramcontent.com/pod-product-compliance
Lightning Source LLC
Chambersburg PA
CBHW060246030726
47493CB00025B/2800